This Little Princess
story belongs to

. . . .

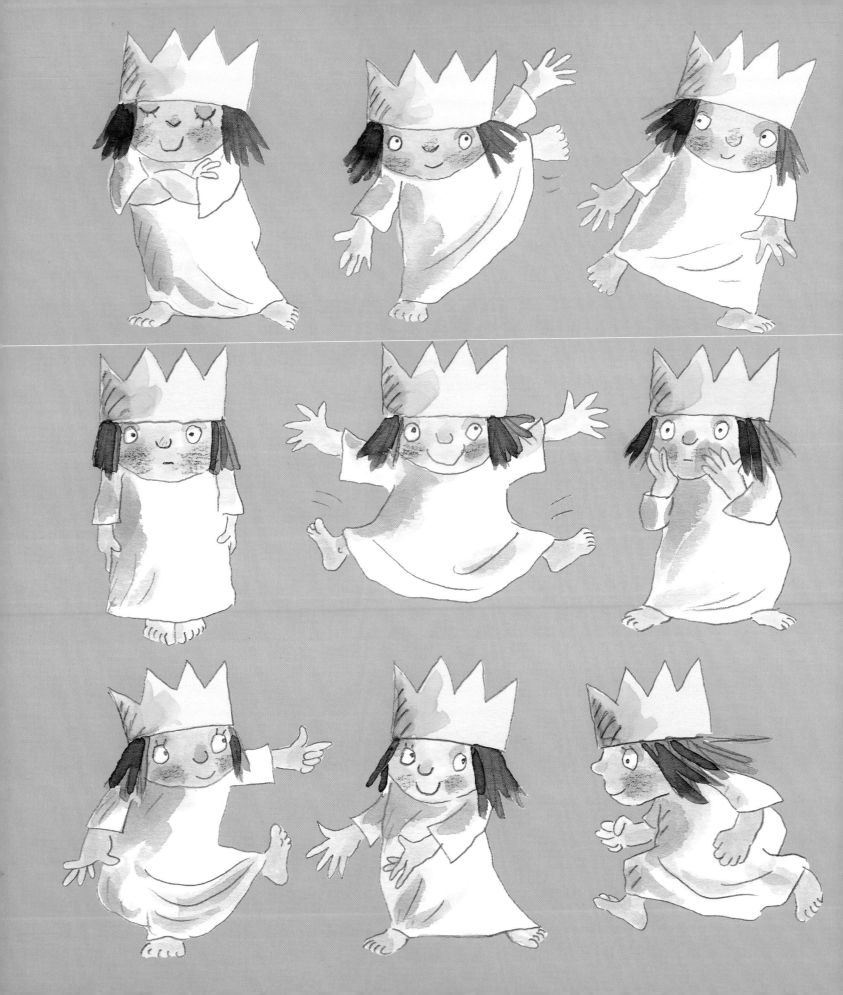

This paperback edition first published in 2014 by

Andersen Press Ltd., 20 Vauxhall Bridge Road,

London SW1V 2SA.

Published in Australia by

Random House Australia Pty., Level 3,

100 Pacific Highway, North Sydney, NSW 2060.

First published in Great Britain in 1995 by Andersen Press Ltd.

Copyright © Tony Ross, 1995.

The rights of Tony Ross to be identified as the author and illustrator

of this work have been asserted by him in accordance

with the Copyright, Designs and Patents Act, 1988.

All rights reserved.

Colour separated in Switzerland by Photolitho AG, Zürich.

Printed and bound in Singapore by Tien Wah Press.

10   9   8   7   6   5   4   3   2   1

ISBN 978 1 78344 013 9

A Little Princess Story

I Want My Dinner!

Tony Ross

Andersen Press

"I WANT MY DINNER!"

"Say PLEASE," said the Queen.

"I want my dinner . . . please."

"Mmmmm, lovely."

"I want my potty."

"Say PLEASE," said the General.

"I want my potty, PLEASE."

"Mmmmm, lovely."

"I want my teddy . . .

. . . PLEASE," said the Little Princess.

"Mmmmm."

"We want to go for a walk . . . PLEASE."

"Mmmmm."

"Mmmmm . . . that looks good."

"HEY!" said the Beastie.

"That's MY dinner."

"I want my dinner!"

"Say PLEASE," said the Little Princess.

"I want my dinner, PLEASE."

"Mmmmm."

"HEY!" said the Little Princess.

"Say THANK YOU."

Other Little Princess Books

I Didn't Do it!

I Don't Want to Go to Hospital!

I Don't Want to Wash My Hands!

I Want a Friend!

I Want a Party!

I Want a Sister!

I Want My Dummy!

I Want My Light On!

I Want My Potty!

I Want My Present!

I Want My Tooth!

I Want to Be!

I Want to Do it By Myself!

I Want to Go Home!

I Want Two Birthdays!

Little Princess titles are also available as eBooks.

LITTLE PRINCESS TV TIE-INS

Fun in the Sun!

I Want to Do Magic!

I Want My Sledge!

I Don't Like Salad!

I Don't Want to Comb My Hair!

I Want to Go to the Fair!

I Want to Be a Cavegirl!

I Want to Be Tall!

I Want My Sledge! Book and DVD